Brood
BROTHERS

JOHN GORDON

Illustrated by
ANN JOHNS

HEINEMANN · LONDON

First Published in Great Britain 1991
by Heinemann Young Books
an imprint of Reed Consumer Books Ltd
Michelin House, 81 Fulham Road, London SW3 6RB

LONDON   MELBOURNE   AUCKLAND

Reprinted 1994

ISBN 0 434 97661 X

A CIP catalogue record for this book is available at the British Library

Produced by Mandarin Offset
Printed in Hong Kong

A school pack of SUPERCHAMPS 13-18
is available from
Heinemann Educational Books
ISBN 0 435 00092 6

Chapter 1
The Dying Tortoise

When Aunt Laura spoke, she puckered her lips as if she was trying to kiss a budgie through the bars of its cage.

'Isn't it a heavenly day?' she twittered.

Alec thought that being sat on by an elephant might be more heavenly than having to stay at The Willows with Aunt Laura, but he said nothing.

'And today,' said Aunt Laura, keeping the corners of her mouth closed and speaking only through the little chirrupy bit in the middle, 'we've all got something to look forward to, haven't we?'

Like mumps, thought Alec. Seeing his cousin Adrian was not exactly like Christmas. He looked down at his breakfast plate, but his sister Judy was polite. She always was when they were staying with Aunt Laura.

'I like Adrian,' she said, which was overdoing it, even for her. 'He's very nice.'

'Everybody says so.' Aunt Laura beamed. 'And he's become *so* handsome – but perhaps his mother shouldn't say that.'

'I agree,' said Alec, and his aunt looked sharply at him. 'I mean I agree he's handsome. Much handsomer than me. Probably.'

'You're still far too young for it to matter,' said Aunt Laura, 'but Adrian is fifteen now, and at that age people take notice.'

Judy was fourteen. She glanced quickly at Alec just in case he said something to make her blush. He often did. But something alarming had happened to him. His eyes had become slits, his mouth was tugged down at the corners, and he was stretching out his neck so that it was thin and scraggy.

'Is he ill?' Aunt Laura was startled. 'Is he having a seizure?'

'No such luck,' said Judy.

'I *beg* your pardon, dear!' Aunt Laura's thin eyebrows hooked themselves high in her large face.

'I think he'll recover,' Judy said.

They watched as the stringiness disappeared from Alec's neck, and then his tortured face lost its lines of suffering and his eyes flickered and opened wide. He gazed from his aunt to his sister like a person coming out of a dream.

'I was just wondering,' he said, 'what it felt like to be a dying tortoise.'

If they had been at home, Judy would have given him a taste of what it felt like to be a dying Alec, but strangling a young brother was out of the question at The Willows, so she said, 'Boys do that sort of thing, I'm afraid.'

Aunt Laura breathed in sharply. 'Adrian never did anything at all like that!'

'No,' said Judy. 'I don't suppose he did.'

'It's because he's at boarding school, you see,' said Aunt Laura. 'It makes all the difference.'

Judy looked down miserably. Why did Alec have to give Aunt Laura so many chances to show how different everything was at The Willows? And why couldn't Mum hurry up and have her baby so they could get back home?

'What's wrong with him now?' Aunt Laura was alarmed.

Alec's head had fallen forward and sagged against his chest. His tongue lolled out a long way.

'Alec!' Judy cried in despair.

He raised his head. 'I'm the tortoise's best friend,' he said. 'I'm dying in sympathy.'

Aunt Laura stood up. 'Well, it's an extremely gruesome sight.' Her bulk rose so majestically that Alec thought of a whale breaking the surface of the sea. He got up too. As he did so, he couldn't help performing the death agony of a

whale with its young – until one of his sad flippers, which was waving the world goodbye, was suddenly grabbed by Judy and he was yanked into the hall.

'I don't know what you think you're doing!' she hissed.

He began to tell her about whales.

'I don't want to know!'

'Let go,' he said. 'You're hurting.'

'Only if you promise.' She flung his hand away. 'Promise you'll stop making those awful faces – please!'

He held his wrist out. Her nail had scratched him. 'That's blood,' he said. 'You've cut the main artery to my heart. I'm dying.'

'You always are!' she cried. 'That's all you ever think about – dying whales, dying tortoises!'

'Well it's more interesting than living

tortoises.' His neck went stringy again and he very slowly raised one leg. 'I ain't even taken a step yet,' he said, 'and that's a tortoise gallop.'

'Stop it!' Judy was in despair. 'I can't stand any more!'

At that moment the outer door opened and a tall figure stood there.

Chapter 2
Adrian

COUSIN ADRIAN STEPPED forward. He
was tall. He was so neat, he gleamed.
He smiled at Judy and ignored Alec
altogether. 'You must be my cousin
Wendy,' he said.

Judy nodded, too shy to correct him.

'Wow!' said Adrian, and undid his
blazer. 'Little Wendy! I don't believe
it.'

Judy began to blush.

'Excuse me,' said Alec.

Adrian looked down at Alec. 'And
you must be . . . ?'

'Alec,' said Alec.

'What seems to be the trouble, Alec?'

'I'm not in trouble.'

'The leg,' said Adrian, pointing. 'It doesn't seem to reach the ground.'

Alec realised he still had one foot clear of the floor, doing the galloping tortoise. 'I been wounded,' he said. 'I just been beaten up.' He looked at Judy as he winced, lowered his foot and took a painful step.

'Looks bad,' said Adrian.

'I'll get over it,' said Alec, bravely limping. 'In time.'

But Adrian was again looking towards Judy. 'You were just a little girl when we last met, Wendy,' he said.

'Yes,' said Judy, shyly.

He smirked. 'I don't know where they've been hiding you all this time, Wendy.'

'I do,' said Alec. 'She's been in prison

for beating people up.'

Adrian raised an eyebrow. 'Are you sure he's your brother?'

'I'm afraid so,' said Judy.

'I think there's something you should know,' said Alec.

'What's that?'

'You're talking to the wrong girl. She's not Wendy.'

'Good grief!' cried Adrian. 'Is that true, Wendy?'

She nodded.

'This is so embarrassing!' said Adrian. 'Please tell me what I must call you.'

'Her real name is Mrs King,' said Alec, 'and she's got a baby in a pram outside.' He threw away his limp and streaked for the open air.

Chapter 3
Blood Brothers

THE SUN SHONE and the garden was huge, but Alec felt like a pebble rattling around in an empty drum. There was nothing to do, and Adrian was a blot on the landscape.

'He can't have much of a brain,' Alec said to himself, 'because she's not even pretty. And he don't know her nasty

habits – not yet.' That cheered him and he crossed the lawn with a lighter step.

There was one good thing about staying with Aunt Laura, and that was her vegetable garden. It was a challenge, because it lay behind a high brick wall, and Aunt Laura had a fierce gardener, Mr Robertson, who kept the gate

locked. Alec, however, knew the loose brick where he hid the key, and in a few moments he was inside.

A blackbird went skittering along the path ahead of him. It was after the same thing as himself – strawberries. But Mr Robertson had been too clever for it, and the strawberry beds were netted.

Alec was reaching under the net when the blackbird's shriek made him jerk his head up. Then he saw he was not alone. There was a greenhouse in the far corner, and behind the glass a figure was moving. Mr Robertson must have had another key.

Alec lowered the net and crept backwards. But he was too late: he had been spotted. Mr Robertson was stalking him, crouching so low that only his head showed above the greenhouse benches.

Alec moved fast. He reached the gate and was about to swing it open when he looked back. The figure was moving between the tomato plants, and he could just see the top of its head. It was not Mr Robertson's bald patch. It was a boy's spiky black hair.

'Hey!' Alec shouted. 'What d'you think you're doing?'

Quicker than the blackbird, the hair flicked out of sight.

'You better come out,' Alec yelled. 'I got a gun.'

'Show us it!'

Alec thought quickly. 'I got this garden surrounded,' he called. 'SAS.'

'Where's your helicopter?' said the voice, and it sounded quite cheerful.

'We're from Scotland Yard,' Alec corrected himself, and lowered his voice to a growl. 'We'll smoke him out, chief.

Send over the tear gas.'

He lobbed a handful of gravel to where the head had vanished – but then gasped as he saw that the stones were heading for the greenhouse roof. The pebbles rattled like gunfire on the glass, and under cover of the noise the cornered culprit made a dash for the garden wall.

Alec was quick to spot his plan. An apple tree grew against the wall with its branches spread out like a ladder. He charged straight through the bean rows and got there just as the boy was on the second rung.

Alec leapt and grabbed an ankle. The boy kicked, and Alec came away with one of his trainers. He leapt again, caught the ragged edge of a pair of jeans and pulled. It was enough. The thief lost his grip and fell.

Alec landed flat on his back and the intruder came down on top of him with a thud that took Alec's breath away. He also had a terrible feeling that something internal had been damaged.

For a moment they lay entangled, but then the boy levered himself up and sat back on his heels. He looked down at his shirt. There was a spreading stain across his chest and something was oozing through the cloth. 'Now you've done it,' he said.

Alec, still gasping, looked down at himself. His own shirt was stained red. He got himself up on one elbow. 'It's my rib,' he said. 'I've busted it.'

But the boy was more concerned with himself. He was looking inside his own shirt. 'It ain't your rib,' he said. 'It's me. Look.' He put his hand inside and brought it out, dripping.

Alec got to his knees. 'I'll get an ambulance,' he said, but then he stopped with his mouth open, for the boy had once more dipped inside his shirt and this time he came out with a ghastly handful of redness. Alec watched in horror, but the boy did not immediately keel over. He lifted his hand and licked his fingers.

'Raspberries!' cried Alec. 'Your shirt's full of 'em!'

'Me intestines,' said the boy, gazing at the red mush. 'I'm dyin'.'

At that moment Alec realised he had found someone who knew how to behave in a tight corner. 'I got hit, too,' he said, gazing down at his bloodstain.

'Looks fatal,' said the boy, and fished inside his shirt and came out with a more or less uncrushed raspberry and handed it over like a grape to an invalid. Alec took it, and they sat cross-legged, each dipping into the shirt as they recovered from their wounds. There was silence until the boy, allowing Alec to have his turn, said, 'That one in me belly-button's mine.'

Alec handed it to him with red fingers. 'I been thinking,' he said. 'I reckon you and me have become blood brothers.'

'Fighting side by side,' said the boy, 'and both of us mortally wounded.' He collapsed in a gory heap and Alec

joined him, stretched out on the gravel.

'What's your name?' the boy asked.

'Alec,' said Alec, not for the first time that morning. 'What's yours?'

'Fergus.'

'Tough luck.'

'It's better'n Alec. Alec sounds like

someone being sick.'

'Fergus sounds mouldy,' said Alec.
'Like furry fungus,' and they were
fighting for possession of Fergus's loose
shoe to club each other when the sound
of voices sent the pair of them shinning
up the tree.

Just before he slid down the ivy on
the other side of the wall Alec caught a
glimpse of Judy at the garden gate.

'Who was it?' Fergus wanted to
know.

'My sister.'

'Well why are we running?'

'Anybody'd run if they saw *her*.'

'Is she ugly?'

Alec stared at Fergus, and Fergus
stared back through the hair that hung
like brambles over his eyes. His brown
face was patched a darker shade where
dust clung to raspberry juice. 'She looks

just like you,' said Alec. 'Horrible.'

Fergus swung at him with his shoe and they went yelping down the slope together.

Chapter 4
Trapped

THEY COULD SEE the spire of the village
church over the trees. 'That's where I
live,' said Fergus, 'most of the time. I
like the woods best.' He led the way
through the trees to a little river.

'That must be my auntie's river,' said
Alec. It ran along the bottom of the
garden.

'I ain't going to steal it,' said Fergus.
'I just want to borrow a bit for a
minute.' He took off his shirt. 'If I don't
clean up before I get home I'll get
tortured.'

'Me an' all.' Alec looked down at his clean shirt blotched with red. He dipped it into the water. 'I reckon that's going to be real blood if my auntie catches me. She's posh.'

'Is she the one who talks like this?' Fergus pushed out his lips as he spoke.

'That's her.'

'Like she's trying to kiss a chicken's bum without touching the feathers.'

Alec had to attack, because she *was* a relative. He used his sopping shirt as a weapon; and their jeans were soon so wet that they might just as well have fallen in, so they did.

'It's a good job skin is waterproof,' said Alec as they hauled and twisted their jeans before they hung them on a high branch in the sunshine. 'I shouldn't like to be wrung out.'

'If skin wasn't waterproof,' said Fergus, 'you'd go soggy like rice pudding.'

'You'd leave great squelchy footprints.'

'Bits would drop off.'

'You'd wear your legs down and go all mushy like my cousin Adrian.' Alec was on his knees, doing a legless walk, when there was the thud of running footsteps, and thrashing through the

bushes came Adrian himself. And just behind him, guarding her face from the whipping branches, was Judy.

'Now I've got you!' Adrian yelled, but he was wrong about that because, like a pair of seals, the two boys had splashed through the shallows to deeper water.

Adrian pulled up at the brink. 'You've been pinching my fruit!' he yelled.

'No we haven't,' said Fergus. 'I never laid a finger on your rotten raspberries.'

'Proof!' Adrian was triumphant. 'I never said a word about raspberries. Thieving and trespassing. And now an offence against public decency.' He hadn't recognised Alec without his clothes. 'How did you get in here anyway?'

'I live here,' said Alec.

'Ha!' cried Adrian in scorn.

'And we wouldn't be indecent if you'd let us get our clothes.'

'Confiscated,' said Adrian, 'to pay for stolen raspberries. Off you go.' He was waving them away when Judy came up and tugged at his arm. 'That one,' she said, 'is my brother.'

'That very skinny one?' said Adrian. 'Who's his horrid little friend?'

'I don't like to look,' said Judy.

Adrian began to laugh. 'Well whoever he is, they make a rotten pair of crooks.' He bundled up their clothes and dropped them into the river. He was still laughing as he and Judy wandered off together.

Chapter 5
The Wooden Horse

LUNCHTIME WAS AWKWARD –
particularly when Adrian said
something about finding waterbabies at
the bottom of the garden.

Aunt Laura raised her eyebrows.
'Waterbabies?'

Judy frowned at Adrian, but Alec
didn't trust him to stay quiet. 'Aunt
Laura,' he blurted out.

'Yes, dear?'

Alec said the first thing that came
into his head: 'I've got a friend who
lives in the village.'

'Have you, dear? Is he a nice boy?'

'Have some *raspberries*,' said Adrian nastily.

'I was just wondering,' Alec said quickly, 'if he could come and play with me this afternoon.'

'I can't have any rough games in my garden,' said Aunt Laura.

'I was just thinking we could walk about and look at the flowers and things.'

'Have some *more* raspberries,' said Adrian, but Alec slipped away and ran off to the village.

Fergus would only enter the garden over the wall. 'Coming in through the front gate makes me feel kind of naked,' he said.

'I wish you'd shut up about being naked,' said Alec, 'I've had enough of that from Adrian.'

'He ain't hardly human,' said Fergus. 'I don't see what your sister sees in him.'

Alec had to stand up for her. 'She's just saved my life,' he said. It was Judy who had smuggled him indoors and got him into dry clothes before Aunt Laura found out. 'We got to save her from horrible Adrian, and I got an idea how we can do it.' His face became serious. 'But it's very dangerous.'

'It don't matter to me,' said Fergus, who had run into deeper trouble when he got home. 'I got nothin' to live for.'

They melted into the bushes and made their way around the lawn to a little wooden summerhouse that overlooked the river. 'This is where we're going to do it,' said Alec. 'We're going to scare Adrian to death.'

'He wasn't very scared of us this morning,' said Fergus.

'That was in daylight.' Alec looked carefully into Fergus's eyes, weighing him up. 'What we're going to do is entice him down here after dark and lie in wait for him in here – in a place where he can't see us.'

Fergus looked around. The summerhouse was quite bare. 'There ain't nowhere to hide,' he said, but Alec pressed his foot down on one of the floorboards and, as he did so, the other end of the board rose an inch. Fergus instantly knew what to do. He got his fingers underneath and lifted. The floorboard came free.

'I noticed that the other day,' said Alec. 'All we got to do is hide under there and come out in ghost costumes with rattles and whistles an' that.'

'I ain't heard of ghosts that whistle.' Fergus was looking into the gap. 'And

anyway there ain't room for both of us.'
He stepped in, and his foot was only a
few inches below the level of the floor.

'I didn't think of that.' Alec looked
down gloomily, but then his face lit up.
'That's only earth down there,' he said.
'We got to dig.'

The idea appealed to Fergus. 'We'll be
convicts,' he said, 'digging our way to
freedom.'

'Prisoners of war tunnelling out
under the eyes of the watchtower.'

They made a lightning skirmish to
the walled garden and came back with a
handfork and a trowel belonging to Mr
Robertson, and soon there was a pile of
loose earth on the summerhouse floor.

'What are we going to do with that?'
said Fergus. 'We can't just leave it there
for him to trip over.' And it was obvious
that fetching Mr Robertson's

wheelbarrow would arouse suspicion, so they sat back and thought. But only for a moment, because the same blinding idea came to both of them:

'The Wooden Horse!'

They remembered the British prisoners digging a tunnel out of their camp from beneath a wooden vaulting horse and spilling out the earth where it wouldn't be noticed. 'We got to make some little bags,' said Alec.

'We ain't got time.' But suddenly Fergus reached into his pocket and came out with a piece of string. He knelt and began to tie it around Alec's leg, just below the knee. 'Now the other one,' he said, 'and I'll fill you up.'

Alec looked at the heap of damp, black earth. 'I don't fancy this much,' he said.

'When the Queen hears about it,' said Fergus, 'you'll get the VC.'

So Alec undid his zip, and Fergus approached with a full trowel, inserted it in the opening and let the earth shoot in. Alec gave a little cry of horror, then clenched his teeth and gazed to heaven like a secret agent in a torture chamber.

'Which way did that one go?' Fergus asked politely.

'Mostly left,' said Alec, and winced as the next cascade evened things up.

'Wriggle it around,' Fergus advised, 'then you won't look so lumpy.'

'Watch where you're putting that thing!' Alec gasped as the trowel entered again and the level mounted.

'It's spilling out. Open your legs and I can get a bit more in.'

'No!' Alec yelled. 'I won't be able to get me zip done up.' He hauled at the tag. It gave a grating sound, but gradually he got it to the top, and then

he looked at Fergus. 'I hope you've got some more string,' he said. 'I ain't going to be the only walking flower pot around here.'

Stooping was difficult, but he managed to tie up Fergus and ladle him full. Then the two human sandbags waddled down to the river's edge where they tugged at the strings and kicked out sprays of earth as they regained a normal shape below the waist.

It took them more trips than they had bargained for, but they had dug out a very satisfactory cavern and there was just one more load of earth, which Fergus had taken aboard, when they stepped out of the summerhouse – and straight into the arms of the dreaded camp guard.

Chapter 6
The Mole

'SO THERE YOU are,' said Aunt Laura.
'I've been looking everywhere for you.'

'We've just been sheltering,' said
Alec, and dropped the trowel into the
grass behind his back. 'We thought it
looked like rain.'

'Silly boys,' Aunt Laura laughed.
'There isn't a cloud in the sky.'

But there was a cloud now because
Aunt Laura, feeling jolly at having dear
Adrian at home, had made a special tea
for Alec and his nice little friend. 'It's
yummy raspberry jam,' she chirped.

Fergus made a clumsy attempt to escape, but as he had to shift so much earth in his bulging trousers he stumbled and Aunt Laura caught at his hand. 'Whoops!' she hooted, and led him indoors.

Alec could do nothing but watch, and he screwed up his eyes in sympathy as Fergus edged himself to his seat by the table and sat down. The unhappiness that spread over his face whenever he had to move meant that Alec was constantly leaning forward to offer him bread and butter, cakes and jam like someone fussing over an elderly relative. Aunt Laura thought this was very sweet and smiled constantly at both of them.

It was all going quite well when Fergus had an uncomfortable sensation in his trouser leg and realised that a worm was taking a stroll somewhere in the region of his right kneecap. Without thinking, he reached down and began to scratch.

A faint pattering sound made Alec think that rain was, after all, falling from a blue sky . . . until he realised it came from under the table. He leant over and saw particles of earth emerging from Fergus's trouser leg and dancing from the toe of his shoe to patter on the kitchen floor.

The look of alarm that crossed Alec's face made Fergus realise that his scratching had loosened the string. He clutched at his leg, but the little stream of earth continued. Desperate measures were needed. He groaned suddenly, clutched at his knee and began to limp from the kitchen.

'Good heavens!' Aunt Laura cried. 'What's wrong?'

'I got cramp.'

'He's got to get out into the fresh air,' said Alec quickly. 'That's the only thing that'll cure it.' He stooped, also clutching at Fergus's knee, and the pair of them had almost reached the door when it opened and Adrian, with Judy behind him, looked down at them.

'What an ugly sight,' he said, but a moment later it was even uglier, for at the sound of his voice the pair of them jerked upright and the string around Fergus's leg gave way completely.

There was a rushing sound, as though a sudden thaw had set in and heavy snow was sliding from the roof, and Fergus's foot disappeared under a pyramid of soil.

Alec was always proud of what he did next. He turned towards Aunt Laura with a face brimming with gentleness and said, 'It's his pet mole. It ain't happy in daylight so he's got to keep it in the earth.'

'Up his trouser leg?' said Adrian.

'He's got to be kind to it,' said Alec.
'It's dying.'

It was the wrong word. He saw his
sister's face, and neither he nor Fergus
stayed to argue.

Chapter 7
The Letter

THE LETTER THAT was going to entice
Adrian to the summerhouse was Alec's
department. Judy wrote letters to
everybody when she was on holiday so
it was easy to get a sheet of her pink
notepaper and an envelope and smuggle
them down to the summerhouse.

Dear Adrian, he wrote.

'That ain't no good,' said Fergus.
'Nobody starts a love letter like that.
You got to say *darlin'* at least, probably
something worse.'

'*My* darlin', then,' said Alec.

'That's getting closer,' said Fergus, 'but I reckon you got to be yukkier.'

'You could slap in another *darlin'*.' Alec looked at the ceiling and moaned, 'My darlin' darlin' Adrian.'

Fergus had his tongue out and was making sick sounds. 'Perfect,' he said, but Alec was carried away and clasped his hands under his chin: 'My darlin' darlin' Angel-Wangel,' and they both rolled on the floor until they had to get serious again.

My darling darling Adrian, Alec wrote, *I am just dying to see you again.*

'Dying is good,' said Fergus.

. . . and if I don't I shall die, Alec added.

'I should put in a bit about a thousand deaths there,' said Fergus.

. . . and if I don't I shall die a

thousand and one deaths for certain.
Alec looked up, got a nod from Fergus,
and wrote: *So if you don't turn up at*
the summerhouse tonight . . .

'. . . when the church clock chimes
midnight . . . ' Fergus added.

. . . *you will find me stretched out*
dead.

They read it through:

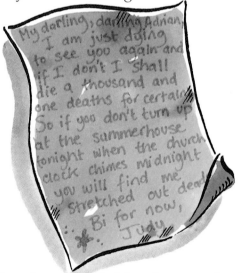

'She always ends like that,' said Alec,
'so that proves it's genuine.'

Chapter 8
Ghosts

THE MOON WAS hidden in the trees
when Alec at long last crept downstairs,
edged open the kitchen door and stepped
into the garden. The shadows were deep
and, even though he was expecting it, he
jumped when he heard the rustle of
Fergus climbing over the wall. On such
a night they would have no difficulty
with a wimp like Adrian.

'I hope I ain't come all this way for
nothing,' said Fergus. 'Are you sure he
got the letter?'

Alec's bedroom was next to Adrian's and he had listened carefully when Adrian came up to bed. 'He got it all right. I heard him swear when he tripped over it.'

'You don't trip over a *letter*,' Fergus complained.

'You do if you put it on a pile of shoes just inside the door. I had to make sure he got it. And I heard him sort of gasp when he read it. He was choking with emotion.'

'So would I have been,' said Fergus, 'if I'd just broken me leg.'

The garden crawled with shadows and they fled to the summerhouse. The black pit beneath the floor looked less inviting than ever when Alec shone his torch. Fergus had brought the white sheet they needed and they draped it over their heads and sank down, lowering the board back in place above them.

'I don't think much of this,' Fergus whispered, crouching in the earthy dark. 'It's too much like being buried alive.'

'Sh!' Alec was listening. 'I can hear someone.'

There seemed to be a rustling from outside, but it ceased.

'How will we know it's him anyway?' said Fergus.

'He'll talk to the moon or something,' said Alec. 'They always do if they're in love with somebody.'

Again the shuffling sound came and was choked off suddenly. They crouched quite still under the sheet, and soft footsteps trod on the boards over their heads.

The sound ceased, and the silence was
like a huge weight above them. They
waited, trying not to breathe, and when
someone spoke they both jumped.

'O Judy,' said Adrian's voice, 'where
are you?'

Silence.

'You wrote to me,' sighed Adrian,
'but now I only have the moon to
talk to!'

This was the moment. They gathered themselves, pressed suddenly against the board above them and shot up through the floor, moaning horribly as they rose.

To make it even more ghastly Alec had switched on the torch so that the sheet would glow with a ghostly whiteness. It would have worked perfectly except, as they shot upwards, the sheet caught on a nail and remained beneath the floor as they rose above it.

However, gambling that the sight of two figures like themselves appearing from nowhere must have been frightening enough, Alec flashed his torch around the room and both of them let out a sobbing shriek.

But their cry died away, for what the torch showed was not Adrian. It shone on something that was not human at all.

In the shadows against the wall, a long white shape stood looking at them. And then, as they watched, it drifted towards them, giving out a piercing wail as it came.

Alec and Fergus did not remember clawing towards the door or fighting their way into the open. The grass barely touched their feet as they ran,

and they flung themselves into the
bushes, tripped and fell, and clung
together, shaking.

Nothing followed them. But a new
sound made their scalps creep.
Laughter. Someone was laughing in the
summerhouse. And it sounded like
Adrian.

Chapter 9
Love Stuff

NEXT MORNING ALEC and Fergus were lurking gloomily in the shrubbery when the sound of Adrian's voice came from the summerhouse. He was with Judy.

'So I dressed up in a sheet and scared the living daylights out of the pair of them.' Even his laughter brayed down his nose. 'Hwah, hwah! And all because they sent me this ridiculous note.'

In the silence as Judy read it Alec and Fergus crept closer and heard her murmur, 'How embarrassing!'

'All that stuff about dying gave it

away,' Adrian chortled. 'Hwah, hwah! Although I do know that young Adrian's fatal charm has captured yet another girl's heart. Am I right, Judy my poppet, or am I right?'

Judy had had enough of his boasting. 'Wrong,' she said.

'Hurray!' cried Alec before he could stop himself.

Adrian's eyes glinted with spite as he lunged forward and snatched them both inside the summerhouse. 'I'm going to make an example of you two!' he snarled, but at that moment Alec gave a heart-rending moan and slumped against Fergus.

'Coward!' cried Adrian, pushing back his sleeves.

Fergus looked up at him with a tragic face.

'Alec's ill,' he said mournfully. 'He's got a terrible disease.'

'What disease?' sneered Adrian.

Alec's tongue lolled out and his eyes were crossed. 'It's something I caught off you,' he said. 'I'm dying of love.'

Rage made Adrian stamp the floor, but he chose the wrong place. His shoe

came down on the loose floorboard and
his foot disappeared into the hole. He
fell forward just as the other end of the
board rushed up at him like a long lost
friend and kissed him with a slap that
sent him flying.

Alec and Fergus raced for the trees.